HAIR-POCALYPSE

written by GEOFF HERBACH

illustrated by STEPHEN GILPIN

Capstone Young Readers
a capstone imprint

Hair-pocalypse is published by
Capstone Young Readers
1710 Roe Crest Drive
North Mankato, MN 56003
www.mycapstone.com

Library of Congress Cataloging-in-Publication Data is available
on the Library of Congress website

ISBN: 978-1-62370-884-9 (paper over board)
ISBN: 978-1-5158-1411-5 (library binding)

Summary: Aidan Allen and his hair do not get along.
In fact, his hair has taken over. Will Aidan be able to
defeat his hair and take back his life?

Designed by Aruna Rangarajan

Printed and bound in the USA.
010467F17

JJ
HERBACH
GEOFF

For my mom, who had a grubby kid. — G.H.

For my sister, Sarah. My main mane wrangler. — Stephen

Aidan Allen was a grubby kid. His clothes were always **wrinkled**, his shoes were always **untied**, and he always seemed to have grass stains on his knees. But none of that was the problem.

The real problem was that Aidan Allen's hair was COMPLETELY out of control. It wasn't just messy. It seemed to have a mind of its own.

"LiE DOWN, HAiR! WHY CAN'T YOU BEHAVE?"

His hair seemed to MOVE.
His hair seemed to SHRUG.

That is NOT possible,
Aidan thought.

Aidan reached into a drawer and pulled out his mom's big blue brush. But when he brushed, the bristles immediately became tangled in his greasy locks. His hair seemed to be GRABBING the brush.

At the breakfast table, Dad looked up from
his phone and shook his head in dismay.

"Aidan, your hair is crazy. You have to do SOMETHING."

"I already tried," Aidan said.

"Better try again," Dad said.

Just then the school bus honked its horn in front of Aiden's house.

"There's just no time," Aidan said as his hair grabbed his spoon and dumped his cereal on the floor!

On the bus, Aiden's hair tied itself into **three bows**. Aiden knew everyone was staring at him. He tried to pretend nothing was happening.

But at school, Connolly Benton spotted Aidan and his crazy hair right away. It had formed **airplane** wings on the sides of Aidan's head. There was NO WAY Connolly would stay silent.

"Look at Aidan Allen's hair!" she shouted.

But from the first bell on, his crazy hair did ANYTHING but stop.

During art class, Aidan's hair grabbed some paintbrushes and splattered paint everywhere!

At lunch, Aidan's hair formed a giant, dangerous **raptor** that blew over Noah Foster's milk — right onto his pants.

"STUPID, STUPID HAIR!"

At recess, Aidan's hair turned into an **octopus-like** creature. It wrapped around Connolly Benton and her friends and yanked them into a nearby mud puddle.

"YOU'RE THE WORST HAIR IN THE WORLD!"

After recess, Aidan felt defeated, and his hair was WORSE THAN EVER. Telling his hair what to do wasn't working. Yelling at his hair wasn't working either. He took a **big breath** and talked to his hair.

Immediately his hair formed into a magnificent mass of curls.

Then it formed a long ponytail blowing in some imagined wind.

Then it rose up into a GREAT, SHINY MOHAWK.

Then it fell into a flowing mullet.

"So you want to be styled? NO WAY!
There has to be another way
to make you happy," Aidan said.

For a moment, there was silence.
Then a bit of air moved through his hair.

On the bus ride home, Aidan and his hair discussed a plan to fix their issues. Aidan was exhausted. Clearly his hair was **exhausted**, too. It lay lifeless and flat, looking even worse than usual.

That night, Aidan took a shower before his dad asked him to. He sang a song and sudsed up.

Aidan and his hair had come to an **agreement**. Aidan would wash every weekday, but weekends were his days to be TOTALLY GRUBBY.

At the breakfast table the next morning, Dad looked up from his phone and shook his head in amazement.

"Your hair looks FANTASTIC!"

"Thanks!" Aidan replied.

"But your shirt is dirty and your shoelaces are untied," his dad said.

"I'm a grubby kid, Dad. I'm doing the best I can right now."

"Gotcha, buddy," Dad said.

Then Aidan Allen and his
hair headed to school —
a little less grubby and
a lot more confident.